Mira and the Big Story

Laura Alary

Illustrated by Sue Todd

Illustrations by Sue Todd. These hand prints were created from carved linoleum and then scanned and colored. www.suetodd.com

www.skinnerhouse.org

Printed in the United States

ISBN: 978-1-55896-693-2

4 3 2
23 22 21

Library of Congress Cataloging-in-Publication Data

Alary, Laura.
  Mira and the big story / Laura Alary.
      p. cm.
  Summary: Curiosity leads Mira into the territory of people whose beliefs are different from hers, but when an "enemy" helps her return home, Mira has big questions that Old Alfred answers with a story showing how all people are connected.
  ISBN 978-1-55896-693-2 (pbk. : alk. paper) 1. Unitarian Universalist Association—Doctrines--Fiction. [1. Toleration—Fiction. 2. Faith--Fiction. 3. Storytelling—Fiction.] I. Title.
  PZ7.A31525Mir 2013
  [E]—dc23
                              2012031002

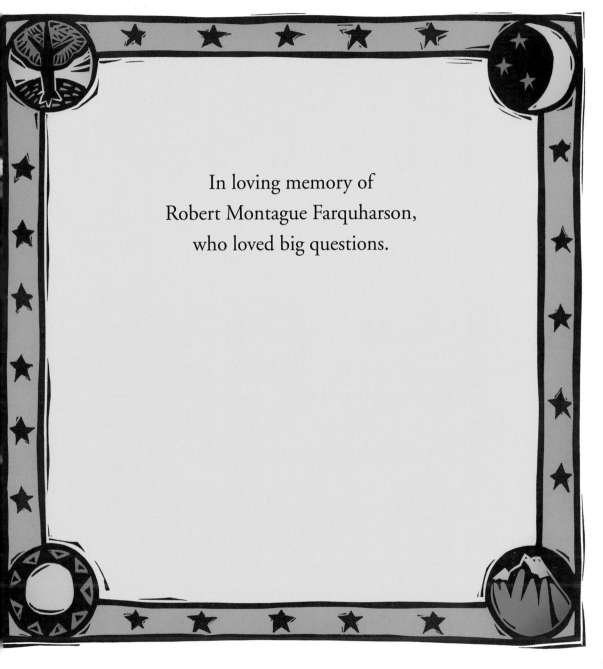

In loving memory of
Robert Montague Farquharson,
who loved big questions.

There was once a green valley that lay between two mountains. Through the valley flowed a river. On each bank of the river stood a village.

As long as anyone could remember, the people of the two villages had been enemies. Strange as it seems, it all began with a couple of stories.

In both villages, the people loved to tell stories. They told stories to amuse themselves, to teach their children, and to help themselves remember important things. Most important of all were the wonderful tales they told about the beginning.

In the beginning, said the people of one village, there was no valley at all—just a flat, rocky plain. When the King of Heaven looked down on the earth and saw people wandering around homeless, he decided to give them a place to live. So he sent enormous birds to gather the rocks and pile them into mountains. Between the great ridges, the birds scratched and clawed a channel that filled with rainwater and became the river. Finally, one of the birds led the people to their new homeland. And that, declared the villagers, is how our ancestors came to this valley. Now it belongs to us—a gift from the King of Heaven.

In the village across the river, a different story was told. Long ago, said the village folk, the Queen of the Earth searched high and low for the perfect people to make their home in the valley. When she found them at last, she sent giant turtles to carry the new settlers up the river on their backs. And that, declared the villagers, is how our ancestors came to this valley. Now it belongs to us—a gift from the Queen of the Earth.

Day after day, year after year, the people of each village told and sang their own stories until they could no longer imagine the beginning of life in the valley any other way. On opposite sides of the river, when the villagers looked across and saw others celebrating a different story of the beginning, they became angry.

"That is not how the story goes!" they all complained bitterly. "This is our valley. It was a gift to us. We belong here. There is no room for the Others."

In a little yellow house in one of the villages lived a girl named Mira. Like all the children in her village, Mira had grown up hearing stories about the beginning. She knew them by heart. She knew the valley belonged to her people. She knew the Others were enemies. She knew they did not belong. But she was very curious about them.

On fine afternoons, Mira often climbed a tree close to the river and watched the people in the other village. Once or twice, when she was feeling especially bold, she even walked far down the bank to a place where the river was narrow and shallow, and waded across.

On the other side, everything was strangely familiar: the trees, the wildflowers, the songs of the birds and insects, the smell of the wind. It was so much like home. Mira looked across the water toward her own village. It felt strange to see it the way the Others did.

On one of these secret visits, Mira was getting ready to cross back over the river when she fell and cut her foot on a rock. She had scarcely sat down when she heard the rustle of leaves. A small boy scrambled down from the tree where he had been hiding.

"Are you hurt?" the boy asked. "How can I help you?"

Mira was too surprised to answer. The boy came closer and held out his hand.

"Here," he said, "take my arm. Lean on me until you get back across."

Together they waded through the water to the other shore.

"Who are you?" Mira wanted to know. "Where did you come from?"

"Where do you think?" the boy answered with a smile.

"Do you suppose you are the only one who is curious about the folk on the other side of the river? I watch you the same way you watch us. But you were the first to cross over. That was brave." He looked at Mira admiringly. "I must go now. I hope we meet again." And away he went.

Mira felt jumbled up inside. For the rest of the day she wondered about the boy. He seemed like an odd piece in a jigsaw puzzle. He was the wrong shape and she could not make him fit. The Others were not supposed to be kind. The Others were not supposed to be curious. The Others were not supposed to be like her. Could the stories be wrong?

There was only one person to whom Mira could bring such a big question.

Old Alfred lived near the river in a stone cottage filled with books. When he was not reading, he was out working in his garden, growing vegetables and herbs from which he made soups, teas, and medicines for the people of the village. Children were welcome to come and pick his raspberries. Old Alfred always offered them homemade cookies and a glass of lavender lemonade. He was wise and kind and his mind and heart were as open as his front door.

That very evening, Mira went to see Old Alfred. She found him enjoying a pot of tea in the garden. He welcomed her warmly and offered her a cup. When Mira was settled with her tea and cookie, she took a deep breath and said, "Old Alfred, I need your help. I have a big question and there is no one else I can ask."

Old Alfred put down his teacup. "A big question, you say. I like big questions. It's been a long time since anyone has asked me a good one. Tell me about yours."

Mira told Old Alfred everything: about her secret trips to the other side of the river, about the boy she had met, and how he was like a puzzle piece that did not fit. Old Alfred listened carefully. Then he asked, "So, what is your big question?" In a small voice, Mira said, "Are the stories wrong?"

For a few moments, Old Alfred stared silently up into the night sky. Then he said,

 "Mira, let me tell you something about stories. Stories can make you bigger—not on the outside, of course, but on the inside. They can stretch your mind and heart. But a story can make you smaller if it takes up all the space in your mind and heart. When new people or new ideas come along there is no room for them. Whenever you hear a story you must ask yourself: What is this story doing to me? Is it making me bigger or smaller? Our village is dear to me, Mira. But our minds and hearts need to be stretched so we can make room for others."

Old Alfred sighed. "There will never be peace in this valley until the people in both villages find a story big enough for all of them."

Mira felt even more mixed-up than before. "I don't understand," she said. "What kind of story could be big enough for everybody?"

"I have a story to share," replied Old Alfred, "if you would care to hear it."

"I would," said Mira.

So Old Alfred began.

"In the beginning there was nothing—yet there was everything. Do you ever collect chestnuts in the fall, Mira? Imagine holding a chestnut in the palm of your hand. Now imagine something even smaller than that little nut containing everything that exists. It was there, but it was not yet there—the way a bright sunflower is and is not inside the striped seed, the way a song is and is not inside the wooden shell of a violin.

Then there was light. Not ordinary light, like the light of stars or candles or a winter bonfire. This was pure energy. Out of it came unimaginably small bits of matter—the first stuff. Some matter came together and formed stars. Over ages and ages, the stars burned, vast furnaces forging new things deep in their hearts. When the time came for them to die, the stars exploded. All the stuff inside them was scattered into space. It drifted like dandelion seeds on the wind, ready to start something new.

From that stardust came everything: clouds and comets, whales and wildebeests, rattlesnakes and redwood trees, emus and elephants, dinosaurs and dragonflies, pussy willows and plesiosaurs, seahorses and stars. From that stardust came galaxies and solar systems and a little blue planet called Earth.

From that stardust came the mountains and the valley and the river and two villages.

From that stardust came an old man and his garden and a girl named Mira and a boy who is still a stranger.

We all come from the same place and we are all made of the same stuff.

We are neighbors on this little planet of ours, sailing through the cosmos."

Mira felt like her mind and heart were so full they would burst.

"If this story is true," she cried, "then no one owns the valley and we all belong here.

If this story is true, the people across the river are not Others. They are like us.

If this story is true we are all connected to each other and to everything else—the river, the trees, the sky, the ocean, the animals.

If this story is true we have wasted too much time being enemies."

Mira began to cry.

Old Alfred said gently, "Mira, tell me what is in your heart."

"What about our stories?" Mira sobbed. "What about the birds who led us to the valley? What about the King of Heaven? What about our gift?"

"Dear child," answered Old Alfred, "you asked me a big question. Now I will ask you some: Who dreamed everything when there was nothing? Whose hand held that little chestnut? Who first lit the stars? Who opened the heart of that little boy to be kind to his enemy? Who opened your mind to see him as someone like you? Who made you so wonderfully curious? Mira, you have not lost your gift, or the One who gave it. Both are just so much greater than you ever dreamed."

Old Alfred handed Mira a large handkerchief to dry her tears. When she was calm, he asked, "So, my dear, what do you think of this story? What does it do to you?"

Mira pictured the face of the boy across the river. She wanted to find him again and learn his name. Maybe they would become friends. Maybe other children would cross the river. Maybe some grownups would come too. Mira felt bigger inside.

"I like your story," she replied with a moonlit smile. "I think it is big enough for everyone."

"Well then," said Old Alfred, "perhaps you can share the story with someone else."

"I will," promised Mira, getting up from her chair. "I already know where to start."

"I thought you might," smiled Old Alfred. "Now get yourself home to bed."

"But Old Alfred," answered Mira, stretching out her arms to take in the whole valley and the sky above, "I already am home."

Then Mira headed out into the starry night.